CAST OF CHARACTERS

Dorothy	JUDY GARLAND
Professor Marvel	FRANK MORGAN
Hunk	RAY BOLGER
Zeke	BERT LAHR
Hickory	JACK HALEY
Glinda	BILLIE BURKE
Miss Gulch	MARGARET HAMILTON
Uncle Henry	CHARLEY GRAPEWIN
Auntie Em	CLARA BLANDICK
Toto	TOTO

and THE MUNCHKINS

The WIZARD of OZ
Movie Storybook

By Jan Wahl

A GOLDEN BOOK • NEW YORK
Western Publishing Company, Inc., Racine, Wisconsin 53404

INTRODUCTION

L. Frank Baum's book *The Wonderful Wizard of Oz* was published in 1900. It has sold over seven million copies and continues to enchant generation after generation of readers. This great book is full of fantastic inventions and surprises. It is truly for the young at heart.

In 1939 Metro-Goldwyn-Mayer decided to bring this magical story to an even wider audience. They released the Technicolor adaptation of the book and did the almost impossible: The movie improved upon the already much-loved story.

Called "the happiest film ever made," MGM's *The Wizard of Oz* is just that. Nobody who has seen it in a theater or on a television screen can forget the joy, the bounce, and the energy of this movie for all ages. Its many songs are forever in our hearts and minds, "Over the Rainbow" in particular. The glow of the Yellow Brick Road, the shimmer from the Emerald City, and the sparkle of the ruby slippers are visual delights never surpassed.

The Wizard of Oz has made itself ageless. It is fifty years young, and this is no wonder, judging from all the hard work and effort that went into making the movie. It took ten writers to write the screenplay and four directors to direct it. There were one thousand fantastic costumes and sixty dazzling sets. The movie was in production for two years.

And, of course, there are the characters. Inspired by the film *Poor Little Rich Girl*, in which various people in the heroine's "real" life appear as other characters in her nightmare or dream, screenwriter Noel Langley had Professor Marvel appear in many guises and at last as the Wizard. Almira Gulch, the nasty schoolteacher, later becomes the Wicked Witch. The clumsy farmhands Hunk, Hickory, and Zeke become the faithful companions the Scarecrow, the Tin Man, and the Cowardly Lion.

Who can forget Jack Haley as the shiny Tin Man? Or Ray Bolger as the kindly Scarecrow? Bert Lahr as the lovable Cowardly Lion? Margaret Hamilton as the awful Wicked Witch? Frank Morgan as the bumbling Wizard? Billie Burke as the beautiful Good Witch Glinda? And, best of all, Judy Garland as Dorothy, through whose eyes we meet them all?

It is Dorothy who inspires us to join her over the rainbow in a land called Oz, and to follow the Yellow Brick Road on a journey that is more real, and more memorable, than anything else we might think of. Let's begin!

ONCE UPON
A TIME IN
KANSAS…

a girl named Dorothy ran down a dry country dirt road.

"I won't let Miss Gulch take you away, Toto!" she cried to her little dog. "I won't!" She looked behind her anxiously, then turned and ran toward the farmhouse where she lived with Aunt Em and Uncle Henry.

"Miss Gulch says Toto chased her cat," Dorothy said breathlessly.

But Aunt Em and Uncle Henry were very busy. "Dorothy, we're counting chicks," said Aunt Em. "We'll talk about it later."

The three hired hands didn't have time to listen, either.
"Look," said Hunk, "you aren't using your head about Miss Gulch.
Don't go near her place and Toto won't get into trouble."

Zeke was driving pigs into a pen. "Hey, kid," he said. "You
going to let old Miss Gulch scare you? You've got to have courage!"

Hickory gave Dorothy a quick glance. "Have a heart," he said.
"We have a lot of work to do."

Dorothy thought no one really cared.

"Someday," she said to Toto, "I'll find a place where we can't get into trouble. It's not a place you can get to by boat or train. It's far, far away—behind the moon, beyond the rain, maybe over the rainbow."

Just as Dorothy was thinking about the place over the rainbow, Miss Almira Gulch pedaled madly into view on her bicycle.

"That dog's a menace to the community!" she told Aunt Em and Uncle Henry. "Here's the sheriff's order allowing me to take him. Hand over that dog!"

Although Uncle Henry and Aunt Em tried to argue Miss Gulch out of it, the paper was legal. "We can't go against the law," said Aunt Em. She was forced to let the old witch have Toto as Dorothy cried and cried.

However, Toto was a smart little dog and managed to escape from the basket Miss Gulch had put him in. He ran all the way home to Dorothy's open arms.

"We've got to get away before she comes back for you, Toto!" Dorothy decided. She gathered a few things and, with Toto, began to walk farther and farther away from the farm. After a few miles she came to a bridge over a gulley.

Dorothy saw a painted wagon. Written on it was, "Professor Marvel. Let him read your past, present, and future in his crystal."

"Little girl, you're running away!" announced a friendly old man as he came out of the wagon.

"How did you guess?" gasped Dorothy, stepping up to him.

He put on his all-seeing turban. "Professor Marvel never guesses. He knows! I'll bet they don't understand you at home and you want to visit other lands with big cities and big mountains!"

"Why," said Dorothy, "it's almost as if you could read my mind."

The old man happened to see a snapshot in Dorothy's basket. Then he gazed into his crystal ball.

"I see a house with a picket fence and a barn," he said. "And a woman in a polka-dot dress. She is worrying about you."

Dorothy was in awe. "That's Auntie Em!"

"That's short for Emily," muttered the professor.

"Amazing," said Dorothy. "What's she doing now?"

"Why," exclaimed Professor Marvel, "she's putting her hand on her heart. She's in pain...."

"Oh, no!" shouted Dorothy. "I've got to go back. Maybe she's sick. Do you suppose she is?"

Just then a big dark wind started to blow. Dorothy thanked the man and rushed off. A twister was drifting over the fields toward her farm. The professor ran for cover.

Hickory, Zeke, Hunk, Uncle Henry, and Aunt Em were also running for cover back at the farm. "It's a twister!" somebody shouted. "Get to the storm cellar!"

"Where's Dorothy?" cried another.

"Henry, Henry!" yelled Dorothy's aunt. "I can't find Dorothy. She's out in the storm!"

Just then Dorothy arrived back at the house. "Auntie Em, Auntie Em!" she called, not knowing that everyone had run to the cellar.

Suddenly a window popped out and struck Dorothy on the head. Then the house seemed to whirl upward and upward into an endless black sky.

"We must be caught in the cyclone," said Dorothy. Then she fell fast asleep from the knock on her head.

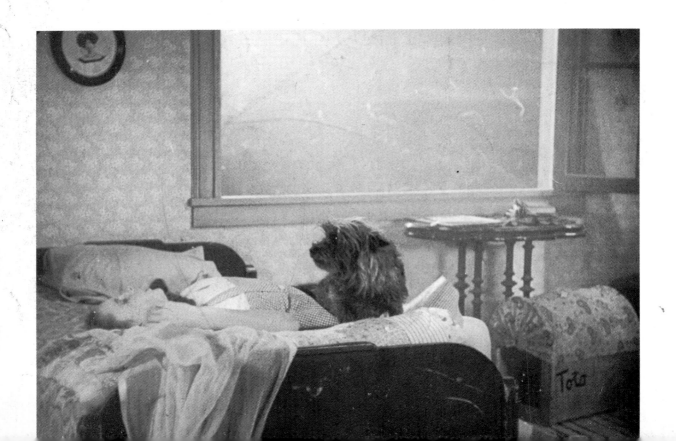

The house landed with a great thump, and Dorothy woke up on her bed with Toto beside her. Gingerly she put her feet on the floor, and then she opened the door and walked outside.

"Toto," she murmured, "I have a feeling we're not in Kansas anymore."

Dorothy stared at her glorious surroundings. "We must be over the rainbow." Suddenly a large shimmering bubble appeared in the air, coming closer and closer. "Now I'm sure we're not in Kansas," said Dorothy.

A very beautiful lady in a long gown stepped out of the bubble, waving a wand. "Are you a good witch or a bad witch?" she asked.

"Who, me?" said Dorothy. "I'm not a witch at all. I'm Dorothy Gale, from Kansas."

"Then is this the witch?" asked the lady sweetly. She was pointing at Toto.

"Absolutely not," said Dorothy.

The lady replied, "But one of you has killed the Wicked Witch of the East by dropping a house on her."

"I didn't mean to do it!" cried Dorothy, who was suddenly startled as many strange small people came out of hiding.

"Who are they?" she asked.

"They are the Munchkins, and you are in Munchkin Land," explained the lady. "I'm Glinda, the Good Witch of the North, and you are their national heroine."

With much pomp and ceremony the Munchkins marched around, inspecting Dorothy from all sides. "She fell out of a star named Kansas," the Munchkin mayor declared, "and killed the Wicked Witch of the East!"

"Ding! Dong! The Wicked Witch is dead," the Munchkins sang as they celebrated, until suddenly there was a roaring flash of red fire.

The frightened little Munchkins flattened themselves on the ground. Waving a broomstick, a hideous green witch stood on a roof and screamed, "Who killed my sister? Was it you?" She pointed at Dorothy.

Dorothy trembled. "No, no. It was an accident. I didn't mean to do it."

"You didn't mean to do it," mimicked the Wicked Witch.
"Well, well, my pretty," she shrieked, "I can cause accidents, too!"

"I thought she was dead," whispered Dorothy to Glinda.

"That was her sister. This is the Wicked Witch of the West,"
said Glinda. "She's much worse."

Glinda turned to the Wicked Witch. "Aren't you forgetting
about the ruby slippers?" she asked.

Glinda raised her wand and—
poof!—the shoes vanished from
the dead witch and reappeared on
Dorothy's feet. "There they are,
and there they'll stay!" declared
Glinda.

"Give me those shoes!" screamed the Wicked Witch.

"Rubbish," said Glinda. "You have no power here. Now go, before somebody drops a house on you, too!"

"All right," said the Wicked Witch. "I'll bide my time. But I'll get you, my pretty, and your little dog, too!"

Then she vanished in a cloud of smoke.

"Which is the way back to Kansas?" begged Dorothy. "I want to go home and I can't go the way I came."

"That's true," said Glinda. "The only person who might know would be the great and wonderful Wizard of Oz himself."

"The Wizard of Oz? Is he good or is he wicked?" Dorothy asked.

"Oh—very good. But very mysterious," answered Glinda. "He lives in the Emerald City. That's a long journey from here."

"But I don't have a bubble or a broomstick," moaned Dorothy.

"You'll have to walk," replied Glinda. "Just follow the Yellow Brick Road."

Dorothy saw that she stood at the beginning of a bright yellow path. Away she went, waving good-bye.

"Now, remember, don't ever take off the ruby slippers or you'll be at the mercy of the Wicked Witch of the West," Glinda called after her.

Dorothy skipped down the shiny road, past hills and valleys, into a quiet cornfield. The only noise was the loud cawing of black crows that picked at the corn. Then all at once she stopped at a fork in the road.

"Which way should we go, Toto?" said Dorothy.

"Pardon me. That is a very nice way," answered a strange voice. It was a scarecrow, flinging out one stuffed arm.

"Scarecrows don't talk," Dorothy declared.

However, when she turned to look and make sure, because, after all, she was over the rainbow, he said, "Of course...the other way is also fine. I can't make up my mind. You see, I haven't got a brain. Only straw."

"I guess scarecrows do talk," thought Dorothy, and she told the Scarecrow that she was going to see the wonderful Wizard of Oz in order to get back to Kansas.

"Take me with you," pleaded the Scarecrow. "Perhaps he can give me a brain. I won't try to manage things, because I can't think."

Dorothy agreed. At first the Scarecrow flopped on the ground, but soon he learned how to walk. Together, Dorothy and the Scarecrow danced down the Yellow Brick Road.

After a few hours Dorothy grew hungry. She noticed an orchard of apple trees off to the side of the road. She ran over and picked a big ripe apple.

"Stop that!" snarled the tree. "How would you like it if somebody picked something off you?"

"Dorothy, you don't want to eat his rotten old fruit anyway," said the Scarecrow.

With that the tree became angry and started throwing his fruit at Dorothy and the Scarecrow. "See, now you can help yourself," said the Scarecrow, laughing. So Dorothy stooped down to pick up an apple and noticed a shiny foot.

"Oilcan!" muttered a rust-jawed tin man.

"Oil can what?" asked the Scarecrow, puzzled.

"Why, it's a man made out of tin," exclaimed Dorothy. "He must mean oil him," she said, and she did.

Slowly the Tin Man creaked to life. "Wonderful!" he exclaimed, moving his elbow. "I've been holding that ax up for a year. I was chopping a tree one afternoon when it rained, and I rusted. I've been that way ever since."

"Well, you're perfect now," said Dorothy.

"Perfect?" repeated the Tin Man. "Hardly. Listen to this!" The Tin Man pounded his empty chest. "I was made very well, but they left out one thing: I don't have a heart."

Dorothy and the Scarecrow looked at each other, then together they said, "Come along! We'll take you to the Wizard at the end of the Yellow Brick Road! He'll give you a heart."

Into a dark forest they trooped—the Scarecrow, the Tin Man, Toto, and Dorothy. "I hope this forest doesn't have any lions or tigers or bears in it," declared Dorothy with a shudder.

They looked around, searching for shadows. Suddenly a horrible roar came out of nowhere, followed by a big lion.

The lion jumped right between the Tin Man and the Scarecrow. "I'll fight you both, with one paw tied behind my back!" he growled. He sprang toward the Scarecrow. "Put up your hands, you lopsided bag of hay!

"Come on," he growled at the Tin Man. "Put 'em up, you shivering junkyard!"

Just then Toto started barking, and the lion began to chase after the little dog. This was too much for Dorothy, and she struck the lion on the nose. "Shame on you," she said.

The lion rubbed his nose and began to cry.

"Why, you're nothing but a great big coward," said Dorothy.

"Is it bleeding?" he asked. "Did you have to go and do that?" the lion sobbed, dabbing his eyes. "You're right. That's what I am—nothing but a cowardly lion. If only I had some nerve."

"The Wizard of Oz can give you courage," said Dorothy gently. "Come with us to the Emerald City."

"Don't mind if I do," purred the Cowardly Lion.

So they all skipped cheerfully down the Yellow Brick Road and were off to see the Wizard, the wonderful Wizard of Oz.

However, unbeknownst to the happy travelers, they were being watched by the Wicked Witch of the West in her crystal ball.

"You won't take warning, eh? When I gain those ruby slippers, I'll be the most powerful in Oz."

So the Wicked Witch set a potion in motion. She chuckled fiendishly, saying, "Now, my beauties! Something with poison in it, I think. But attractive to the eye, soothing to the smell! Poppies! Poppies! Poppies will put you to sleep."

The Emerald City loomed just ahead across a wide field of poppies. "We're almost there! At last!" Dorothy shouted. "It's exactly like I knew it would be. He really must be a wonderful wizard to live in a city like that!"

"Hurry! Hurry!" said the Tin Man, racing forward.

But suddenly Dorothy became very tired. "I can't run anymore." She yawned. "I'm so sleepy. I have to rest."

"You can't rest now," said the Scarecrow. "We're almost there." But Dorothy lay down on a bed of poppies and shut her eyes.

"Come to think of it," added the Cowardly Lion, "forty winks wouldn't be bad."

"Don't you start, too," said the Scarecrow. Then the Tin Man began to cry softly because he also felt too tired to make it across the field. "Don't cry! You'll rust yourself! This is terrible! Help!" shouted the Scarecrow.

The Lion was snoring, Dorothy lay asleep, and the Tin Man was rusting again. The Scarecrow shuddered. "This is a spell. It's the Wicked Witch! We're doomed!" He flapped his arms about in despair.

Glinda heard the cry for help and waved her wand. Snow drifted down on the poppy field and woke the weary travelers.

"Unusual weather we're having, isn't it?" said the Cowardly Lion, stretching.

Soon Dorothy woke up and oiled the Tin Man's limbs, and the group went on its way.

The Wicked Witch saw all this in her crystal ball. "Curses! Curses! Somebody always helps that girl!" She leapt onto her broomstick. "To the Emerald City as fast as lightning!" she ordered. "Woe to those who try to stop me!"

With joy, the companions finally stumbled up to the gate of the Emerald City. Anxiously Dorothy rang the bell. Huffing and puffing, a porter poked his head out the window. "Who rang the bell? Can't you read the notice?" he said with a sigh.

"What notice?" they all asked.

"Why, er—this notice!"

After he hung it out, they read in one voice: "Bell out of order. Please knock!"

So Dorothy knocked. "That's more like it!" yelled the porter. "What do you want?"

Dorothy, the Scarecrow, the Tin Man, and the Cowardly Lion chanted, "We want to see the Wizard."

The porter scoffed. "Nobody can see the great Oz! Nobody! Nohow! Even *I've* never seen him! You're wasting my time."

He started to close the window when the Scarecrow said, "The Good Witch of the North sent us. Look! Dorothy is wearing the ruby slippers!"

"Why didn't you say so? That's a horse of a different color!" said the porter. "Come in! Come in!" He swung the door open and they rushed through.

First they were given a general bath and brushing up after their travels. However, as they came out spick-and-span, they saw the people of the Emerald City staring upward in horror.

On her broomstick, the Wicked Witch was smoke-writing a message in the sky. It said, "Surrender, Dorothy!"

"She's followed us here!" cried Dorothy. "What should we do?"

"Well," said the Scarecrow, "we'd better hurry if we're going to see the Wizard."

They rushed down a long green hall into the vast, awe-inspiring throne room.

Suddenly a voice that shook the polished floor itself boomed, "COME FORWARD!" A huge head appeared in the middle of orange clouds of smoke. The travelers' knees wobbled.

"I am Oz, the great and powerful!" the head exclaimed. "WHO ARE YOU?"

"I am Dorothy, the small and meek. Auntie Em may be sick and it's all my fault. I must get back to Kansas. And the Tin Man wants a heart, and the Scarecrow a brain, and the Cowardly Lion would like to be king of the forest!"

After a moment of silence, there was the sound of thunder as the voice shouted, "The great Oz has every intention of granting your requests. But first you must prove yourselves worthy by performing a very small task."

Dorothy was about to clap her hands with happiness when the voice commanded, "Bring me the broomstick of the Wicked Witch of the West!"

"B-B-B-But if we do that," gasped the Tin Man, "we'll have to kill her to get it!"

"SILENCE!" called the voice of the Wizard. "Now go!"

"But what if she kills us first?" asked the Cowardly Lion.

"I said GO!" shouted the Wizard.

Dorothy and her friends scurried away to get the broomstick as the Wizard had demanded. Pretty soon they found themselves in the Haunted Forest behind the castle where the Wicked Witch lived. The Cowardly Lion read the sign, which said, "I'd turn back if I were you!"

At the same time the witch was watching them in her crystal. "I want those ruby slippers most of all!" she said as she turned to the leader of her army of winged monkeys. Then she screeched, "Fly! Fly! Do as you like with the others, but I want you to bring the girl here alive and unharmed." Off went the evil band.

Down upon Dorothy, Toto, and the others swooped the winged monkeys. They stomped on the Scarecrow, scattering his straw. Dorothy screamed as they lifted her up, quickly carrying her away.

Afterward the Cowardly Lion and the Tin Man put the Scarecrow back together. "We've got to save Dorothy," they agreed as they headed toward the witch's castle.

In the meantime, Dorothy was pleading with the witch to let her go. "You can have your ruby slippers. Just give me back Toto and let us go!" she cried.

"All in good time!" cackled the witch, reaching for the slippers. Sparks flew as she touched them.

"Drat!" said the witch. "I forgot. Those slippers will never come off—as long as you are alive! But how to do it delicately..." she muttered.

Toto saw an open window and managed to escape. He ran from the castle as fast as his little paws would carry him.

"Run, Toto, run!" cried Dorothy.

"Catch him, you fools," the witch yelled to her army.

"He got away," said Dorothy.

"Which is more than you will," replied the witch as she grabbed an hourglass. "When the sands run out, you will die!" Then she left the room.

Toto ran to the Haunted Forest to find the three faithful friends. "Where'd he come from?" asked the Tin Man. Toto kept barking and pulling at their legs.

"Don't you see, he wants to take us to Dorothy," said the Scarecrow, and they followed Toto up the steep rocks.

Disguising themselves as Winkies, the witch's guards, they crept into the black castle.

In the tower, the sands of the hourglass were almost gone. "I'm in here," yelled Dorothy. Her friends heard her, and just as they were all about to escape, the witch and her guards found them.

"Oh, so you want to get away, eh, Scarecrow?" shrieked the witch as she tossed a ball of fire at him.

At once Dorothy grabbed a bucket of water and threw it on the Scarecrow. Some of it splashed on the Wicked Witch and she began to melt. "Oh, what a world, what a world! I'm going!" shouted the witch. "You cursed brat. Who would have thought a good little girl could destroy my wickedness. Ohhhhh!"

Nothing was left of the witch except her hat and broomstick.
"You've killed her!" said the leader of the Winkies.
"I didn't mean to," Dorothy told him. "It's just that the Scarecrow was on fire."
"We don't mind," he said. "She kept us here under a curse."
"Then may I take her broomstick?" asked Dorothy.
"Gladly," replied the leader as he handed it to her.

In triumph Dorothy and her friends took the broom to the Emerald City to present it to the great Oz.

"We melted the witch," Dorothy explained to the fiery orange head. At the same moment, Toto had discovered a curtain and was tugging it open. Behind it stood a small nervous man who was operating a machine. This was the great and powerful Oz—a mere mortal man.

"So, you've found me out," moaned the Wizard. "Yes, I'm a bad wizard," he confessed. "I don't have any magic." He saw that they were disappointed. "However, I may be able to help you anyway."

"What about my brain?" asked the Scarecrow.

"Here's a diploma," announced the Wizard as he reached into a large bag. "You are now a doctor of thinkology." The Scarecrow quickly calculated the square root of almost anything.

"My heart?" asked the Tin Man. The Wizard explained that he had one already, because a heart is not judged by how much you love, but by how much you are loved by others. The Tin Man looked around at his friends and knew the Wizard was right. Then he gave the Tin Man a red heart-shaped ticking watch to remind him.

"My courage?" asked the Cowardly Lion. The Wizard gave him a magnificent triple cross to wear on his chest, which made him a member of the Legion of Courage.

"And as for you, Dorothy," declared the Wizard, "I'm really from Omaha, which is very near Kansas, and I can take you back with me the same way I came here." He pointed to his hot-air balloon, and they climbed aboard.

Crowds gathered to see them off, but just before they were about to leave, Toto jumped out of Dorothy's arms and she had to get out of the balloon to fetch him. Then suddenly the balloon took off without her.

"Sorry, I don't know how it works!" called the Wizard as he sailed away and out of sight.

"Now I'll never get back to Kansas!" Dorothy sobbed.

"Wait!" said the Scarecrow. "Here's someone who can help you!"

Glinda floated down into the main square in her bubble. She smiled at Dorothy and said, "You don't need help any longer. You've always had the power to go back to Kansas yourself."

"I have?" asked Dorothy. She was puzzled.

"You just had to learn for yourself," said Glinda.

"What did you learn?" asked the Tin Man.

"Well, I think," Dorothy replied, "that it wasn't enough to miss Uncle Henry and Auntie Em. I had to learn that if I ever need to go looking for something again, I shouldn't look any farther than my own backyard."

"Is that it?" asked the Cowardly Lion.

"That's it," answered Glinda. "Now, just click your heels three times and say, 'There's no place like home.'"

So Dorothy hugged all her friends good-bye and then held Toto tight in her arms. "I'll miss you all," she called, "and I'll think of you always. But there's no place like home. There's no place like home."

Dorothy shut her eyes and immediately spun through the air. When she awoke, Aunt Em, Uncle Henry, Hunk, Zeke, and Hickory were gathered around her bed. Even the professor had come to see if she was all right after the storm.

"Auntie Em, Uncle Henry," Dorothy cried. "I'm back!" She tried to tell them about where she had been in Oz, but then she realized they would never understand. Instead, she reached out and hugged them and said, "Oh, Auntie Em, there's no place like home!"